The Feathered Ogre

A Story from Italy

Retold by Fran Parnell · Illustrated by Sophie Fatus

Barefoot Books
step inside a story

Contents

CHAPTER 1

AN IMPOSSIBLE TASK

Long ago in a country far away,
the king was very sick. The royal doctor
came to his bedside. First, he made the
king say, 'Ahhh'.

Then, he counted the beats of the
king's heart. Finally, he shook his head.
'Only a magic feather from the
Ogre's back can cure you, Your Royal
Highness,' he said. All the noble knights
and ladies gasped. They were horrified.

The Feathered Ogre lived on an
island far to the north. Everyone in the
kingdom was afraid of him.

Every year he jumped into a boat
and came to the mainland. He captured
one hundred of the most tasty and
tender young men and women.

He took them back to his island and stored them for food. One year he even snatched the king's older daughter. She had been visiting her aunt in the north.

Many brave men had tried to stop the Ogre. Many set off to the Ogre's den, but none had ever returned.

The very sick king sighed. It was a huge sigh. Then he announced, 'I will give a reward to whoever brings me a feather from the Ogre's back.

'I will give him my beautiful younger daughter in marriage. I will also give him half of my kingdom.'

I don't want to marry!

But in his heart, the king was sad. He did not believe it could be done. And, in their hearts, his people agreed with him. The journey was so frightening. It was utterly impossible to pluck a feather right from the evil Ogre's back.

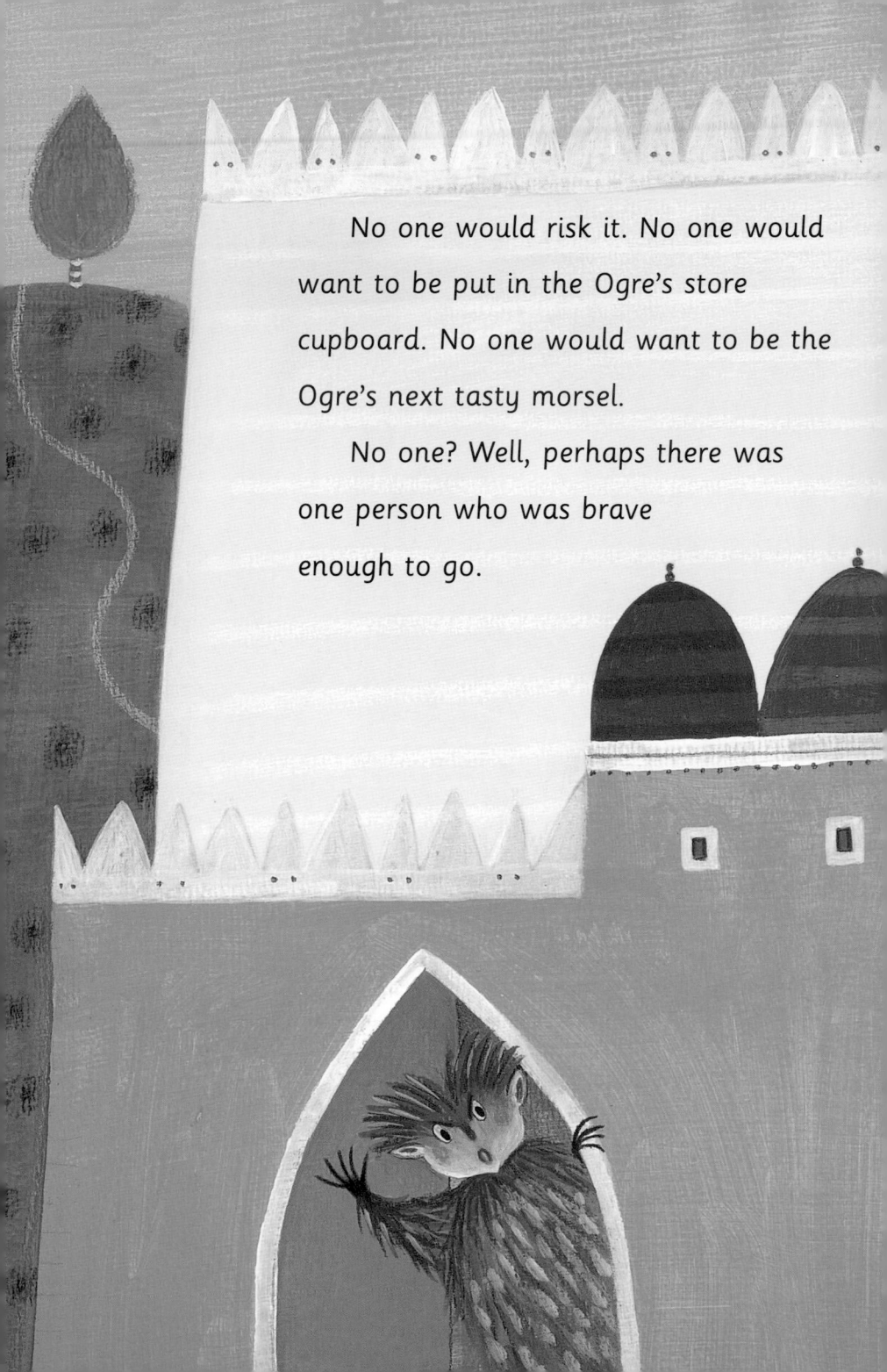

No one would risk it. No one would want to be put in the Ogre's store cupboard. No one would want to be the Ogre's next tasty morsel.

No one? Well, perhaps there was one person who was brave enough to go.

CHAPTER 2

A FrighteNing JourNey

Pírolo was one of the king's gardeners. He was the youngest one. But he was tired of weeding the royal potato patch. He was fed up with picking fat caterpillars off the royal cabbages.

When he heard about the reward,
his eyes became dreamy. He longed for
a wild adventure. He imagined half a
kingdom of his own.

The only bad part was marrying the
younger princess. She always made faces
at him from the palace windows.

However, Pírolo decided to try and get the feather. He threw down his spade and found a strong walking stick. Then he set off to the far north.

Pírolo travelled for many days. He went uphill and he went downhill. He walked through valleys where the grass was as soft as silk and as green as a frog. He walked over rocky cliffs where the rough stones were as lumpy and twisted as a witch's nose.

Finally, he reached the shore at the end of the kingdom. In front of him was the sea.

And across the sea was the Feathered Ogre's island. Pírolo stood there and wondered how he might get across.

Suddenly he heard the splash of oars and a person sighing. The sighs were long and sad.

I am so tired!

A rickety wooden boat was drifting towards him over the waves. In the boat sat the oldest man that Pírolo had ever seen.

His face was as wrinkled as a raisin. He had a long white beard. The tip of it trailed over the side of the boat into the salty water. The boat reached the shore.

Hello, old man!

'Good day!' called Pírolo in a cheery voice. 'Will you row me over to the Feathered Ogre's island?'

The boatman looked at Pírolo with
tired eyes. Then he spoke to Pírolo
with a very tired voice. Pírolo thought
it was the weariest sound in the world.

'Traveller, I have rowed from shore to shore for a thousand years. I am worn out to my bones. The Feathered Ogre has put a spell on me and I cannot get out of this boat. So, sir, it does not matter to me if there is a passenger in it or not.'

Pírolo shook his head sadly at the boatman's gloomy tale. Then he jumped into the little boat.

CHAPTER 3

A HeLPiNg HaNd

When they reached the island, the
boatman pointed to a huge wooden
door. It was set into the cliff nearby.
Pírolo took a deep breath. He knew
what he had to do. He marched bravely
across the sand and banged on the door
with his walking stick.

After a while, the door slowly
creaked open. Pírolo raised his stick
again. He was ready to give the Ogre a
bop on the nose. But it wasn't the ugly
Ogre standing behind the door.

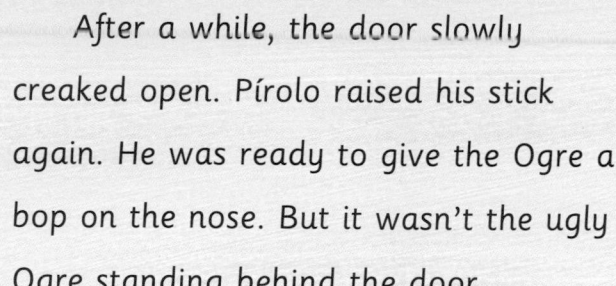

24

Instead, it was a beautiful girl. She had bright blue eyes. She looked at Pírolo with a puzzled frown. 'You're not the Feathered Ogre!' she said. 'Who are you? Why are you here?'

25

Pírolo explained everything to the
girl. She was surprised. 'Why, the king
is my father!' she said. 'That wicked
old Ogre captured me last year when I
was visiting my auntie. He didn't eat me
because I offered to keep his cave spick
and span for him.

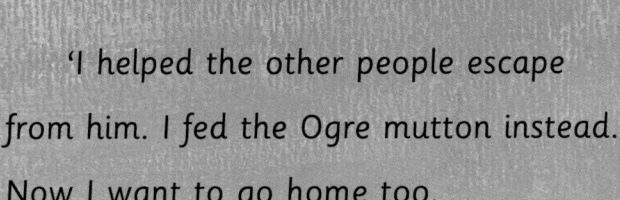

'I helped the other people escape
from him. I fed the Ogre mutton instead.
Now I want to go home too.

'If you help me to find the
way, I will get a feather for you.'
Of course, Pírolo agreed.

I'll
help you

'Come into the cave and hide under the table,' said the princess. 'The Ogre will be back soon!'

Pírolo dived under the table just as the door flew open. The Feathered Ogre burst in.

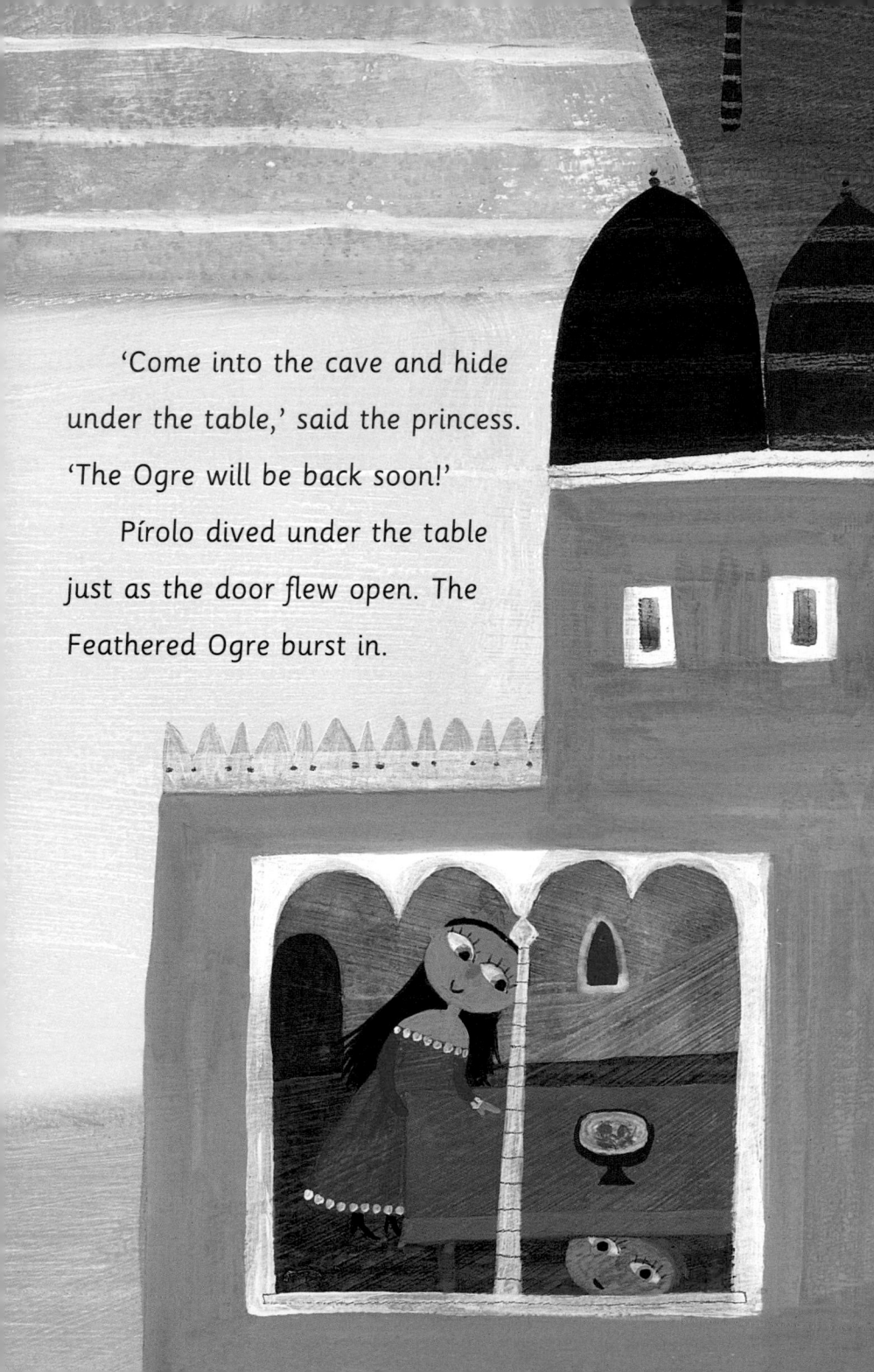

CHAPTER 4

The Ogre's Secret

The Ogre looked horrible. He was scowling. His face was as scrunched as a rotten cabbage. 'Where is my supper?' he shouted.

'Here it is, Ogre dear,' said the princess. 'You munched the last man yesterday. So I have made delicious dumplings for you tonight.'

'Bah!' roared the Ogre. And he stuffed all of the dumplings into his mouth at once. 'Tomorrow I will catch more tasty human beings for my supper.' Then the Feathered Ogre wiped his chin on one feathery arm.

30

'Hah, hah, hah!' he sniggered.
'Every time I sit in the boat with that
old boatman, I laugh to myself. If only
he knew!' And he wiped a tear of
laughter from his eye.

'If only he knew what, Ogre dear?'
asked the princess.

'If only he knew how easy it is for him to escape from my magic! He could be as free as the air. All he has to do is give his passenger the oars to hold and then jump quickly out of the boat. The passenger would be stuck in his place instead.

32

'The passenger would be the
one rowing from shore to shore until
doomsday. Hah, hah, hah!'

Pírolo was listening carefully under
the table.

33

'Ogre dear, you look tired,'
murmured the princess thoughtfully.
'Why don't you have a little nap?'

'Mmmm,' said the Feathered Ogre
with a big yawn. 'That is a good idea.
I am tired out.' And he put his head
down on the table.

The girl stroked the Ogre's feathers and sang to him. Finally, he fell into a deep sleep and began to snore.

The princess quickly pulled a magic feather from his back. She threw it under the table to Pírolo.

'Ow!' howled the Ogre, waking up.

'I've been stung!'

'There, there, Ogre dear,' the
princess said softly. 'It was just a little
spark from the fire that burned one of
your pretty feathers. Go back to sleep.'

'Hmmm,' said the Ogre sleepily. He
put his head back on the table. Soon he
was snoring again.

'Quick!' whispered the princess to
Pírolo. 'Now is our chance. RUN!'

CHAPTER 5

The Great Escape

Let's get out of here!

Pírolo and the princess held hands and ran across the cave. They opened the huge door and rushed outside into the daylight. But the door slammed shut with a loud bang.

Come back here!

As Pírolo and the princess ran towards the boat, they heard the Ogre wake up. 'Aaaargh!' the Ogre raged angrily.

'Row, boatman, row!' cried Pírolo as they flung themselves into the boat. Behind them, the door of the cave burst open and the Ogre charged out.

'Come back!' shouted the Ogre. He hopped up and down in the sand.

But the boatman rowed as if the sea was on fire. At the other side, Pírolo and the princess jumped out safely.

We will be home soon.

Then they told the boatman how to escape from the spell. The boatman smiled for the first time in a thousand years!

Pírolo and the princess ran towards home. The princess clutched the precious feather in her hand. Uphill and downhill they dashed. Finally, they reached the palace.

I am well again!

The magic feather cured the
king instantly. He was delighted
to see his older daughter again.
He even danced a jig around the
throne room.

He kept his promise and gave
Pírolo half of his kingdom. And he
let Pírolo marry the older daughter
instead of the younger one.

Everyone was happy!

43

Everyone? Well, everyone except for the wicked Feathered Ogre. While Pírolo and the princess were running home, the boatman rowed back to the island.

They won't get away with it!

When he got there, the Ogre leaped into the boat with a roar. 'I will catch that nasty pair, you will see,' he shouted. 'Row faster!'

The Ogre was very angry. So he
did not notice the boatman smile.
The boatman said, 'Why don't you
take the oars? A mighty ogre like you
could row much faster than an old
man like me.'

The Ogre did not realise that the boatman knew the secret. The Ogre grabbed the oars and sent the boat skimming over the waves like a bird.

But before he could get out at the other side, the boatman jumped out of the boat into the shallow water.

'Hah, hah, hah!' the
boatman laughed. He clicked his
heels in the air with delight.

'I'm free! I'm as free as the
air!' And he ran away over the
pebbly beach.

The Feathered Ogre howled in horror.
Pírolo and the princess heard it far away
in the palace. Now the Ogre was cursed
by his own spell. He had to row the boat
from shore to shore until doomsday. And,
as far as I know, he is still rowing!